HELLO! WELCOME TO THE FABUMOUSE WORLD OF THE THEA SISTERS!

Hi, I'm Thea Stilton, Geronimo Stilton's sister! I am a special reporter for <u>The Rodent's Gazette</u>, the most famous newspaper on Mouse Island. I love traveling and meeting new mice all over the world, like the Thea Sisters. These five friends have helped me out with my adventures. Let me introduce you to these fabumouse young mice!

Colette has a real passion for fashion. She loves to design her own clothes in her favorite color, pink.

Violet loves studying and learning new things. She is a fan of classical music and dreams of becoming a famouse violinist someday.

Pamela loves pizza so much she eats it for breakfast. She is a skilled mechanic who can fix just about any motor she gets her paws on.

PAULINA is shy and loves to read about faraway places. But she loves traveling to those places even more.

Nicky is from the Australian Outback, where she developed a love of nature and the environment. This outdoors-loving mouse is always on the move.

Thea Sisters

Thea Stilton

MOUSEFORD ACADEMY

SEA TURTLE RESCUE

Scholastic Inc.

Copyright © 2011 by Edizioni Piemme S.p.A., Palazzo Mondadori, Via Mondadori 1, 20090 Segrate, Italy. International Rights © Atlantyca S.p.A. English translation © 2017 by Atlantyca S.p.A.

The publisher does not have any control over and does not assume any responsibility for author or third-party websites or their content.

GERONIMO STILTON and THEA STILTON names, characters, and related indicia are copyright, trademark, and exclusive license of Atlantyca S.p.A. All rights reserved. The moral right of the author has been asserted. Based on an original idea by Elisabetta Dami.

www.geronimostilton.com

Published by Scholastic Inc., *Publishers since 1920*, 557 Broadway, New York, NY 10012. SCHOLASTIC and associated logos are trademarks and/or registered trademarks of Scholastic Inc.

Stilton is the name of a famous English cheese. It is a registered trademark of the Stilton Cheese Makers' Association. For more information, go to www.stiltoncheese.com.

No part of this publication may be reproduced, stored in a retrieval system, or transmitted in any form or by any means, electronic, mechanical, photocopying, recording, or otherwise, without written permission of the copyright holder. For information regarding permission, please contact: Atlantyca S.p.A., Via Leopardi 8, 20123 Milan, Italy; e-mail foreignrights@atlantyca.it, www.atlantyca.com.

ISBN 978-1-338-11658-8

Text by Thea Stilton

Original title *Missione "Mare Pulito"*
Cover by Giuseppe Facciotto
Illustrations by Barbara Pellizzari (pencils) and Francesco Castelli (color)
Graphics by Chiara Cebraro

Special thanks to Beth Dunfey
Translated by Andrea Schaffer
Interior design by Kay Petronio

10 9 8 7 6 5 4 3 2 1   17 18 19 20 21

Printed in the U.S.A.   40
First printing 2017

RETURN TO THE BEACH

It was a peaceful summer night on Whale Island. A perfectly round moon surrounded by twinkling stars shone over Turtle Beach.

Suddenly, there was a ripple of waves on the **SEA**, and two figures slowly emerged from the water. A ray from the moon **illuminated** the wet shells of two large sea turtles slowly making their way to shore.

This was the beach where they had been born twenty-five years earlier. Now they had come back to lay their **eggs**.

Once they'd found a good spot for their nests, the mama turtles dug deep holes and deposited their eggs. Then, as the darkness of **N I G H T** was replaced by the first light of dawn, they covered them carefully and headed back toward the sea.

A few **HOURS** later, an alarm buzzed in a dorm room across the island at Mouseford Academy. Nicky and Paulina woke with a start. The annual international meeting of the **Green Mice Environmental Organization** was about to begin!

This year, the Green Mice meeting was going to be in Finland. Nicky and Paulina couldn't wait to tour the Finnish countryside and **visit** the country's magnificent fjords.

"What do you say we go for a quick swim before we catch our flight?" suggested Paulina as she **FLIPPED** through her Scandinavia guidebook.

Please stay shut!

"**Great idea**," replied Nicky. "I don't know if I'm brave enough to dip my tail into those **icy** Finnish waters!" She flopped down on her enormouse **suitcase** and tried to keep it shut.

The **mouselets** hurried down to Turtle Beach. But when they got there, they noticed strange lines in the sand. They looked like **TIRE TRACKS**.

"Someone drove a car onto the beach!" Nicky exclaimed in alarm.

"But these tracks **lead** straight into the sea. How is that possible?" Paulina asked.

The mouselets followed the tracks down the beach until they reached the place where they disappeared into the sea. They could see that sand had been moved, but they couldn't figure out what had happened to the car.

"Of course!" cried Nicky, SMACKING herself in the snout. "Why didn't I think of it sooner? These aren't tire tracks—they're loggerhead sea turtle tracks!"

How strange!

These tracks remind me of something . . .

Paulina looked at her friend. "Do you think sea turtles came and laid their eggs in the sand?"

Nicky nodded. "They must have made their NEST here."

"We've got to tell Professor Van Kraken right away," Paulina said, pulling out her CELL PHONE.

Half an hour later, IAN VAN KRAKEN, Mouseford's marine biology professor, joined the mice at TURTLE BEACH.

"First of all, we need to fence off this section of the beach," he explained. "The eggs will hatch in about a month and a half, and we've got to protect them from the ELEMENTS."

The professor looked thoughtful for a moment. "It's too bad you two won't be around to help this summer. We'll need volunteers to care for the nest and check the temperature of the sand every day."

Nicky and Paulina exchanged a LOOK.

"Professor, we can do it!" Nicky said ENTHUSIASTICALLY.

"Are you sure? You'd have to cancel your TRIP to Finland," the professor said.

The mouselets nodded.

"We're lucky. We get to travel all the time," Paulina said. "Helping these turtles is the opportunity of a lifetime, and we don't want to miss it!"

ONE MONTH LATER

"There's no point debating it," declared Nicky. "Ratteron's best **DOCUMENTARY** is *definitely* *The Macaque in Love!*"

"Yep, it's one of his most *entertaining* movies,"

admitted Paulina. "But what about *One Spotted Shark?*"

"Well, that one's great, too." Nicky sighed. "I give up. It's impossible to decide which is the best. They're all amazing!"

Colette and Violet exchanged a *smile*.

Nicky and Paulina took their documentaries very seriously! It was nice to see them so excited.

The four mice were sitting in the first row of a large lecture hall. The school year was about to **begin** in a very memorable way: James Ratteron, their favorite documentary filmmaker, would be teaching a **class** at Mouseford Academy!

Over the course of the semester, Ratteron would share his *secrets* for making beautiful documentaries. He was famouse for following the lives of rare animal species on the brink of extinction.

"Violet, Colette, what's your **favorite** documentary?" asked Nicky.

"I liked *The Friendly Cricket*," Violet replied, smiling shyly. She was thinking of Frilly, her pet cRicket.

"Well, my favorite is

FRILLY THE CRICKET

FLAMINGOS

A *Flock of Flamingos*," said Colette. "The colors in that movie are absolutely faBumouse. They are so extraordinarily, exquisitely PiNK!"

The others laughed. Colette always *appreciated* the pink side of everything!

"I'm here, I'm here!" panted Pam, scurrying into the classroom. "Sorry I'm late." She slid into a seat next to her friends.

"Don't worry," Paulina reassured her. "James Ratteron isn't here yet."

"Thank goodmouse!" said Pam, catching her breath. "I've had a really weird morning: Everywhere I went, I ran into the same rodent. He kept blocking my way and getting my paws in a pickle."

"**Who** was it?" asked Violet.

"I don't know," said Pam. "Someone I've **never** seen before."

"A new **student**?" asked Paulina.

"I don't think so," Pam replied. "He had a **video camera**, and he was filming all over campus."

"Maybe he's a journalist who wants to *interview* **James Ratteron**," suggested Nicky.

"Could be," said Pam thoughtfully.

Huh?

I saw him in the cafeteria . . .

Oops!

. . . and outside on the steps, where he was filming insects . . .

Hmph!

WHerever I Went, He Was always bLocKing MY PatH . . .

BANG! Ouchie!

. . . untiL We ran riGHt into eacH otHer!

"As I was **hurrying** over here, I ran right into him. We both ended up tumbling on our tails."

At that moment, the room **exploded** with applause. JameS RatteRON had just made his entrance. Behind him was the *headmaster*, Octavius de Mousus. Next to them was a **young ratlet** carrying a video camera.

"Rat-munching

rattlesnakes, it's him!" Pam cried.

She could scarcely believe her eyes: the ratlet she'd been running into all morning was James Ratteron's **ASSISTANT**!

A NEW FRIEND

After a brief **INTRODUCTION** from the headmaster, James Ratteron took the microphone and began squeaking. He told the students about the **mysteries** of nature and how they'd fascinated him since he was just a mouseling.

I'm so happy to be here!

He'd received his first video camera as a twelfth birthday **gift**. It had immediately become his **inseparable** companion.

When he grew up, he decided to study film. He wanted to show **nature** in all its glory by making wild animals the *stars* of his documentaries.

The students listened to the director with their snouts gaping wide open like a pack of **HUNGRY** cats at feeding time. His **passion** for nature was contagious! The lesson passed in a flash.

At the end of the lecture, Nicky leaped to her paws. "Let's go! We've got to get down to Turtle Beach." She and Paulina *hurried* out.

Colette **WAVED** good-bye. Then she turned to her other friends. "What an AWESOME class, right?" she said.

"Yeah, it made me want to make a documentary," said Shen enthusiastically.

"Me, too," said Violet. "But did you hear how much work goes into every film Ratteron makes? A ton!"

"I know," said Craig. "I thought all you had to do to film animals in their natural habitat was find a really good hiding spot, like behind a tree or something . . ."

"You need a lot more than that," said Pam. "You have to really understand animal habits and the environment. Plus, you need a lot of **patience** and really good assistants."

Pam felt a **tap** on her shoulder. She turned and found herself snout-to-snout with Ratteron's a**ssistant**.

"Hi, I'm Mike," he began. Then he blushed

Hi, I'm Mike!

redder than a golden hamster. "I want to apologize for this morning. I was very **rude**."

Pam *smiled*. "I'm the one who should apologize," she said. "I left without squeaking a word! I hope your **video camera** wasn't damaged."

"Don't worry, I didn't let it hit the ground. This one time in India, a **macaque** swiped it right out of my paws, and ever since then I've been extra careful," Mike said earnestly.

Pam *laughed*.

Mike chatted with the students for a few minutes. He told them his dream was to become a great documentary filmmaker like his **BOSS**, James Ratteron.

After **STUDYING** for the past

few years, Mike felt ready to make his first **documentary**, but he was looking for an original idea.

Violet, Pam, and Colette exchanged a **KNOWING** look.

"We might have the perfect subject for you," said Pam. "Come down to the beach with us. We've got two good FRIENDS you just have to meet . . ."

NEST NANNIES

After James Ratteron's lesson, Nicky and Paulina *hurried* to the beach. For a few **WEEKS** now, they had been going down to check on the turtles' nest every day.

"Good news, Paulina," said Nicky. "The temperature of the sand is the same." She jotted down a few notes.

JULY 9: The nest is protected.

AUGUST 14: The night shift

"This summer has gone by faster than a hamster on a wheel," said Paulina. "Just a few more days and the eggs will hatch!" A **sad** expression flitted across her snout. "I'm going to miss all this."

The two mouselets looked around. The sand glittered beneath the rays of the sun, and the only sound that broke the silence was the gentle lapping of the **WAVES** against the shore. Paulina closed her eyes and took a deep breath of the salty air.

Suddenly, a *shrill* squeak broke the spell.

The temperature is the same!

"Hey, nest nannies! How's it going down here?"

It was Ruby Flashyfur. She was jogging along the shore with her friends the Ruby Crew — Alicia, Connie, and Zoe.

"Are you still all wrapped up in those silly eggs?" Ruby asked with a smirk.

Nicky put a paw on her hip. "Yes, we are. Do you have a problem with that?"

"Oh, no, no problem at all." Ruby giggled. "Fussing over eggs seems like the perfect activity for you . . . EGGHEADS!"

Alicia, Connie, and Zoe snickered together. Then they sprinted off down the beach.

Nicky rolled her eyes. "Sometimes those four rodents are just **the worst**."

"You said it, sis," said Paulina. "But **who cares**? Let's not get our tails in a twist over their silly jokes."

Just then the mouselets heard a familiar squeak:

"Nicky! Paulina!"

It was Pam, Colette, Violet, and Mike SCURRYING to join them.

"Hey, mouselets!" said Paulina in surprise.

"What are you doing here? And what's the big rush?"

"We came to give you some big news," Violet replied. "This is James Ratteron's assistant, Mike. We've told him all about the sea **turtle** nest you're caring for —"

"And GUESS WHAT?" Pamela interjected. "He wants to turn your loggerhead turtles into MOVIE STARS!"

THE FIRST
INTERVIEW!

Mike, Nicky, and Paulina began discussing the project. Together they decided the film should have lots of general *information* about turtles, plus interviews with the rodents taking care of the NEST. It would end with video of the eggs hatching.

"This DOCUMENTARY will be a great way to spread the word about how important it is to protect endangered species," Paulina said. "As the Green Mice always say, 'Nature needs you!'"

AFTER class the next day, Colette, Violet, and Mike climbed into Pam's JEEP and headed south.

Their destination: Tide House, home of Professor Ian Van Kraken's laboratory!

The marine biology professor was the first rodent Nicky and Paulina had turned to when they'd discovered the nest. Mike definitely wanted to interview him for the documentary.

"Welcome, students," said the professor, ushering them into his LAB. "I'm ready to answer your questions."

Mike and the Thea Sisters quickly prepared a small set. Then Mike turned on his video camera and began filming.

"Professor Van Kraken," asked Colette, "would you tell us why your students' work is so IMPORTANT?"

"Of course," the professor began. "Loggerhead sea turtles could become endangered, so it's vital to protect their nests from predators and other threats. New hatchlings are the key to continuing

the **species**."

The mouselets nodded, and Professor Van Kraken continued. "Female sea turtles nest every two to three years. They bury their eggs in the sand. When the eggs hatch, the little turtles work together to dig their way out. When night comes, they **head** toward

SPECIES ID CARD: LOGGERHEAD SEA TURTLE
DIET: Crabs, mollusks, whelks
REPRODUCTIVE SEASON:
The warmest months of the
year, typically June, July, and August
EGG INCUBATION PERIOD: Two months

the sea, using the light of the HORIZON to guide them."

"Extraordinary!" whispered Colette.

"According to studies," continued the professor, "if they aren't DISTURBED, female turtles remember the beach where they were born. They use Earth's magnetic field to find their way back as **ADULTS** when they return to lay their eggs!"

After of the interview, the Thea Sisters helped Mike put away his equipment.

"The professor was absolutely fabumouse," he commented. "Tomorrow we can go film the nest."

"Perfect. We'll **set** up the cameras on the beach," said Pam.

The young mice continued **CHATTING** as they headed back to the academy. They were so busy **talking**, they didn't realize someone was **WATCHING** them . . .

RUBY CREW REPORTING FOR DUTY!

Ruby had overheard bits of the conversation between Mike and the Thea Sisters, and she was more curious than a cat.

"What are they up to this time?" she muttered, turning toward the entrance to the cafeteria. She bumped into Elly, who was hurrying out.

"Hey, watch where you're going!" Ruby snapped.

"Oh, sorry! I was running to Turtle Beach to bring snacks for Nicky and Paulina. I MADE cookies —"

Ruby cut her off. "By the way, do you know what the Thea Sisters are up to? A

Hey!

Oops . . . excuse me!

few minutes ago, I saw them with Ratteron's assistant."

Elly brightened.

"Oh, you didn't hear? Mike wants to make a documentary about the hatching of the baby TURTLES. He asked the Thea Sisters for help."

Ruby's snout fell open in amazement. Before she could squeak, Elly was on her way again. "Okay, I've got to RUN! Bye!"

There was no time to waste. Ruby immediately called an EMERGENCY meeting of the Ruby Crew.

"Can you believe it?" Ruby bellowed as soon as the other mouselets entered her room. "The Thea Sisters are going to be

STARS in a real movie! And it's all because they spent so much time with those silly **eggs**."

From: Ruby

Emergency meeting in my room. SCURRY UP!

"Well," said Connie, "they did spend their entire summer babysitting those turtles. Don't you think they deserve it?"

"What a load of goat cheese!" Ruby replied. "I don't care what they've done. I will not allow the Thea Sisters to become the center of **attention** yet again! Those mouselets are a total thorn in my paw."

"But, Ruby . . ." interjected Alicia, "Nicky and Paula really are environmentalists."

Ruby waved a paw **dismissively**. "Well, then we'll also have to become environmentalists!"

Alicia, Connie, and Zoe looked at her in **surprise**.

"Crew, it's time to listen to your captain," Ruby said. "We can have our cheese and eat it, too. I may not be a great environmentalist yet," she went on, smiling slyly, "but I am a great actress!"

THE RIGHT LOOK

Early the next morning, there was a **KNOCK** at Nicky and Paulina's door.

"It's not even seven," Paulina muttered. She stumbled sleepily to the door. "Who could that be?"

Paulina opened the door and found herself snout-to-snout with a mountain of **clothes**. She could just make out a pair of pink-clad paws.

Help me!

"**HELP ME!**" a high-pitched squeak exclaimed. "Take these. I need to go get some more stuff!"

"Colette?" Paulina asked as she helped free her friend from the pile of clothing. "What is all this?"

"Outfits for you to choose from, of course!" Colette replied. She scurried away and returned a moment later with her paws FULL of makeup and accessories. "Ready to try these on?"

"Um, you want us to try your clothes on?!" Nicky asked.

"Uh-huh," said Colette. "Once we've picked your outfits, then we'll think about your fur-styles and accessories."

"Outfits?" Paulina asked. "Coco, what are you squeaking about?"

"Mouselets, do I really have to spell it out?" Colette asked, grinning. "Today you're being interviewed for Mike's documentary! Don't you want to look your best?"

Nicky and Violet GLANCED at each other and laughed. It was useless to resist Colette once she'd gone into full-on

GLaMorously
Sporty

Vintage AtHLete

STYLiSH Sailor

The right LOOK for a day in the wild!

Casual Chic

Green Mice
Thea Sisters in action!

fashionista mode. So they let their friend get to work.

After a **whirlwind** fashion show of tracksuits, pants, hats, scarves, and earrings, Colette declared herself **satisfied**.

"Now all we're missing is the **FINAL touch**! But where did I put them?" she mumbled. She rummaged through the **PILE** of clothes and extracted two T-shirts with the Green Mice logo on them.

"Ta-da! I added a little **FLAIR** to the Green Mice look," Colette explained. She'd

decorated the shirts with lots of sparkly beads.

"Thanks, Coco!" Paulina said.

"These look amazing," said Nicky admiringly. "They're sporty *and* stylish!"

Nicky and Paulina were finally ready. Mike was waiting for them at Turtle Beach, where Pam and Violet had **SET UP** a small platform for **FILMING**.

At first, Paulina was nervous, but little by little she grew more confident in front of the camera. "Based on the temperature and the type of **SAND** on this beach," she began, "we estimate that the little **TURTLES** will dig their way out —"

"Wait!" Pam cried. She was acting as the sound technician. "I hear **something** . . ."

Violet cocked her snout, listening. "I hear it, too. Someone is singing!"

Four mouselets were approaching, singing at the top of their lungs.

"The Golden Dragonflies, that's our name!
Protecting nature is our game!"

It was the Ruby Crew! Ruby **IGNORED**

the Thea Sisters and went straight to Mike. "It's a pleasure to meet you. I'm Ruby Flashyfur, president of the Golden Dragonflies," she said, shaking his paw. "My friends and I have come to help protect these poor little TURTLES."

"The Golden Dragonflies?!" asked Colette, bewildered. "What's that?"

"Um, yeah, so I PROBABLY didn't have time to squeak to you about it. It's an environmental association sponsored by Flashyfur Enterprises, my mother's company," Ruby said.

"And when was it founded?" asked Pam.

"This summer," Ruby replied quickly. "You see, we SACRIFICED our vacation to help animals at risk!"

Nicky chewed her whiskers. She was suspicious of the Golden Dragonflies'

motives. Knowing Ruby, this was probably an act. But before she could squeak, her **cell phone** began ringing.

"Hello? Professor Van Kraken, what's going on?" she asked. "Of course. We'll be there RiGHt away."

She hung up and turned to her friends. "We've got to get to Tide House. It's an EMERGENCY!"

An Emergency Meeting

Over at the marine biology LABORATORY, the Thea Sisters found Professor Van Kraken, Elly, and Tanja waiting for them.

"We've got a **problem** brewing offshore," said Tanja. "An alarm just went off. There's invasive **SEAWEED** heading our way."

"What does that mean?" asked Colette.

"If **winter** is particularly warm, some species of seaweed will multiply *excessively*," the professor explained. "It can damage the marine ecosystem."

Ruby and her FRIENDS had joined the Thea Sisters at Tide House. "So what?" Ruby snorted. "Why should we care about this weird seaweed or whatever?" Then she realized that Mike was recording this

So what?

scene, and she forced a smile. "Because our little turtles are waiting for us, and we'd like to get back to them."

"That's exactly the problem," Elly jumped in. "The seaweed could land on the west coast and reach Turtle Beach, putting the hatchlings in danger!"

Professor Van Kraken nodded gravely. "Yes, it's true. Once the eggs hatch, the baby turtles could get tangled in the seaweed and become trapped before they make it to the open sea. But

I have a solution in mind. To **protect** the beach, we can install a *floating* anti-seaweed barrier along the coast."

"How would that work?" asked Pam.

Elly went up to the lab's chalkboard and drew a quick sketch. "The barriers will

The hatchlings are in danger!

Yes, it's true . . .

contain the seaweed offshore, keeping it far from Turtle Beach."

"I'll **contact** my colleague at the Marine Observatory on Mouse Island to get

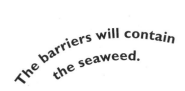

The barriers will contain the seaweed.

the floating barriers," announced Professor Van Kraken.

"Then we'll need to get offshore to set them up," said Paulina.

Alicia stepped forward. "Ruby could loan you her JET SKI . . ."

"Thanks for the offer," Pam said as Ruby glared at Alicia, "but we'll need something bigger to transport the barrier."

There was a moment of silence while everyone thought it over. Then Colette exclaimed, "The fishermice!"

"The FISHERMICE? Do you think they'd help us?" asked Pam.

"We could ask," said Colette. "Let's go find Leopold Whale!"

The Whale family was one of the biggest and oldest families on Whale Island. The Thea Sisters didn't know Leopold well, but his sister, Midge, was the cook at Mouseford and his brother Mercury was the island's mailmouse.

Colette was sure Leopold would help. The Whales were DEVOTED to the island. In fact, some rodents believed Whale Island was named after their family.

WE SET SAIL!

A few hours later, two **fishing boats**, the *Cheddar I* and the *Cheddar II*, were preparing to combat the **SEAWEED INVASION**. At the port, the Mouseford students scurried around, LOADING the barriers onto the boats.

This is heavy!

James Ratteron had joined them, assuring the rodents he would **HELP** in any way possible.

"Long ago, I made a documentary about an **enVirONMeNTaL** threat like this one," explained the director. "Maybe my experience could be useful."

"Okay, the barriers are all **PACKED** on board the fishing boats," said Elly.

"Very good," declared Professor Van Kraken. "Nicky, Mike, and I will go with the **equipment** on *Cheddar I*, while Mr. Ratteron and Paulina will sail on the *Cheddar II*."

"What about us?" asked Ruby, scurrying over. "Who do we go with?"

"You're going to stay here," Pam said hurriedly. "You'll just get in the way."

"Get in the way? **US?!**" replied Ruby. She

was **OUTRAGED**. "Golden Dragonflies, that's our **NAME**! Protecting **NATURE** is our —"

"If you want," interrupted Colette, "you can come with us to Turtle Beach."

"Why?" asked Ruby. She was still offended.

"Professor Van Kraken wants us to

Keep calm and scurry on!

transfer the nest to Seashell Beach to make sure the **turtles** stay safe," Colette explained.

Ruby stared at her for a SECOND. Then she shrugged. "Okay, you go ahead. We'll be right over."

As soon as Colette, Pam, and Violet were gone, Connie turned to Ruby. "But, seriously, do we have to help the Thea Sisters move the nest?" she asked in astonishment.

Were you serious?

"Of course not," Ruby replied. "Who cares about a bunch of turtles? I just want to be the star of the documentary! Let's follow Mike and his video camera. And we don't need a shabby old fishing boat to do it!"

She pulled out her cell phone and dialed her personal assistant. "Alan? Prepare the yacht. We set sail in *ten minutes*!"

We'll follow them on the yacht!

OPERATION BARRIER!

"Cheddar II calling *Cheddar I,* do you hear me? Over!"

Paulina's squeak crackled over the walkie-talkie hooked to Nicky's belt.

Her friend hurried to reply. *"Cheddar I* here, we hear you LOUD and clear. Over!"

"We are in position. Are you? Over!"

"We just REACHED our position. We're about to install the barrier. Over and out!"

The two fishing boats had reached the open sea. Now the crews were preparing for the most delicate PART of the mission: lowering the floating barrier.

Mike set up his video camera's lens to take a panoramic shot. Suddenly, he heard the fluttering of wings. A **SECOND** later, the head of a **GRUMPY-LOOKING** seagull appeared on the viewfinder. It had settled on the rail right in front of him!

"AAAHHH!!!" yelled Mike in surprise, losing his **grip** on his precious **video camera**. It slipped through his paws.

Luckily, Nicky was able to **grab** it.

"I thought you said you two were inseparable?" JOKED Nicky, passing the

video camera back to Mike.

"Yeah . . . that bird almost made me jump out of my fur," said the ratlet, smiling sheepishly.

The walkie-talkie crackled again:

"*Cheddar II* to *Cheddar I*! We finished anchoring the **barrier**. Over!"

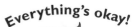

Everything's okay!

Nicky glanced at the stern and caught Leopold Whale's eye. The young fishermouse nodded, letting her know that the mission was complete.

Nicky hurried to respond to Paulina. "*Cheddar I* here! MISSION accomplished for us, too!"

The two crews **burst** into applause. But their celebration was interrupted by a loud *boom* that didn't bode well for the

two small boats.

"We must hurry back to the port!" cried Leopold, looking at the large, dark **CLOUDS** that had thickened on the horizon. "There's a storm coming!"

A storm is coming!

We've got to get back!

STRANDED IN THE STORM

The sky had quickly filled with **DARK** clouds that were so low they seemed to want to squash the **ONLY** boat left at sea: the Flashyfur yacht!

The Ruby Crew's journey to join the **fishing boats** had begun smoothly enough, but soon Alan — who was acting as captain despite his lack of experience at sea — discovered that following the *Cheddar I* and *Cheddar II* was a lot more difficult than Ruby had led him to believe.

If that wasn't bad enough, big, fat raindrops began beating down on them.

Alan suggested returning to the port, but Ruby wouldn't listen to **reason**. She ordered him to **continue**, and so they did.

But as day gave way to night, Alan realized they were lost in the middle of the **sea**.

"I'm sorry, Miss Ruby. No one heard the **SOS** I sent out over the radio!" said Alan, joining the Ruby Crew in the cabin.

"So now what do we do?" asked Alicia.

"As usual, Alan has let me down," Ruby said, sniffing with disdain. "I'll take command of the rudder and figure it out."

SOS!

Alicia, Connie, and Zoe left the cabin. They looked at one another **miserably**.

"**MOUSELETS**, we're in more trouble than a mouse at a cat convention. Ruby doesn't know anything about **NAVIGATION**!" blurted Connie.

Zoe **gazed** at the waves crashing over the surface of the sea. "We're going to have to spend the night in the middle of this **storm**." She sighed. "Unless . . . we could try calling someone from the academy."

We have to do something!

"But Ruby will **NEVER** let us!" exclaimed Alicia.

"Then it'll have to be our **little** secret," said

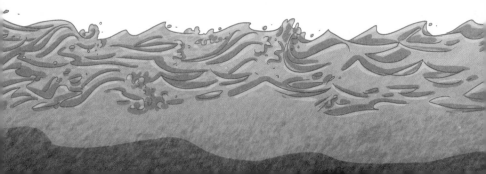

Connie as she took out her cell phone to call Elly. **HoPefuLLy** she and the Thea sisters could **help**!

Call in progress:

ELLY

00:03

A ROUGH RETURN

As they were transferring the sea turtle **eggs** to Seashell Beach, Violet, Colette, and Pam realized a storm was brewing. They **HURRIED** to shelter the nest. They'd seen Nicky and Paulina complete this **T A S K** so many times they knew just what to do.

While Colette and Violet stretched and fastened a weatherproof tarp over the nest, Pam dug a drainage ditch in the **SAND** to collect the rainwater in a spot far from the **NEST**. That way, the nest would stay as dry as possible.

When the nest was secure, Colette, Pam, and Violet **HURRIED** to the port to meet the fishing boats as they returned.

Nicky and Paulina came **ashore**, but their friends barely had a chance to squeak

HELLO before Elly scurried onto the pier, out of breath.

"Hurry!" she exclaimed. "We have to go back out!"

"Elly, what are you talking about? There's a **storm** coming!" said Paulina. "We can't go back out there. It's too **DANGEROUS**!"

"Yeah, that's definitely not a good idea," added Nicky, *shaking* the water out of her fur.

Mouselets, it's an emergency!

"Don't worry about the turtles," Colette put in. "We sheltered the nest and —"

Elly interrupted her. "Mouselets, you don't **understand**. There's no time to lose! The Ruby Crew took the Flashyfurs' yacht out to meet you, and now they're lost at **sea**!"

The **MOUSELETS** quickly scurried back onto the *Cheddar I*.

"I'm coming, too," said Professor Van Kraken. "This could be dangerous. I've done a **RESCUE** like this before. Follow my lead."

What?!

"Will we need special equipment to **REACH** them?" Nicky asked.

The professor nodded. "We can't bring the *Cheddar I* too close to them in this weather. The sea is so choppy, the two boats could crash into each other. We'll have to use a **SMALL LIFEBOAT** to reach them."

The rain was beating down **NONSTOP**. The *Cheddar I* went out at top speed, bouncing over the rough sea.

There's no time to lose!

"We've picked up an **SOS**! They must be close," shouted Pam as lightning TORE through the sky.

"I see them!" cried Violet, pointing at the yacht, which was tossing and turning on enormouse **WAVES**.

The mouselets and Professor Van Kraken left Leopold on board the *Cheddar I* and set off on the lifeboat. A few minutes later, they pulled up next to the anchored yacht. The Thea Sisters reached for their classmates' paws and helped bring the Ruby Crew to **safety**.

"We can come back for the yacht after the storm," the Professor told Ruby.

"Well, thanks for the **HELP**," said Ruby, "even if we were doing just fine by ourselves . . ."

Once the Ruby Crew and Alan were

safely on board the lifeboat, the mouselets made sure everyone was wearing a **life jacket**.

"Are you okay?" Nicky asked Zoe as she helped her **fasten** her jacket.

"Yes, thanks, we're all fine," responded the mouselet. "I've never been so happy to see you in my life!"

A NEST TO PROTECT

As soon as they'd returned to Mouseford, the Thea Sisters, Mike, Professor Van Kraken, James Ratteron, and the other students met in the Lizard Lounge. Everyone was WORN OUT from the rescue, but the storm was still raging and this was not the moment to rest.

"We did good work this evening," James Ratteron began. "Thanks to the *floating* barrier, the seaweed won't reach the beach."

At those words, the students all cheered. The **nest** was safe!

"Wait a SECOND, everyone!" the professor exclaimed. "I love your enthusiasm. But our work is not yet done. The *eggs*

MEETING IN PROGRESS!

could hatch any moment now. The little turtles take at least two days to reach the **surface**. We should take turns keeping an eye on the nest during this delicate period."

"Paulina and I can take the first shift **tonight**," Nicky volunteered.

Craig **stood up**. "You and Paulina have already done **ENOUGH** today. You should rest for a bit."

"Craig's right," said Shen. "You go catch some Z's. We'll take care of the nest."

"Thanks, ratlets," said Nicky gratefully.

We'll do it!

While the others figured out a **SCHEDULE** of shifts to check the **BEACH**, Paulina went to the window. "Let's hope the weather **IMPROVES**. This storm could be a catastrophe for the hatchlings."

Nicky put a paw around her friend. "Don't worry, Paulina. I know our turtles can do it!"

We'll take the first shift.

Operation Nest Watch

- PROTECT THE NEST FROM PREDATORS
- MONITOR THE TEMPERATURE OF THE SAND
- KEEP AN EYE ON THE WEATHER

Schedule of Shifts

WEDNESDAY

NIGHT: ELLY, RYDER

THURSDAY

DAY: RON, TANJA
NIGHT: SHEN, CRAIG

A BITTER SURPRISE

Two days later, a warm golden light filtered through the shutters of Nicky, Violet, and Paulina's room, waking them from a deep sleep.

"Finally, a beautiful day of sunshine!" exclaimed Paulina, JUMPING out of bed and throwing open the window. "Thank goodmouse! I don't think I could stand another gloomy day."

"Me neither," Violet agreed.

"Especially since the first turtles might be born **tonight**," said Nicky, rolling over. She rubbed her eyes and **LOOKED** at the alarm clock on her nightstand. "I know our turn doesn't begin until eight, but I want to

do a quick check of the **beach**. Let's call the others."

"I was just thinking the same thing," replied Paulina, "but I bet Colette and Pam are still **SLeePiNG** . . ."

Just then Nicky's cell phone emitted a

BEEP! BEEP!

From: Colette

Pam and I are up. What do you say we go over to the beach? ;-)

It was a message from Colette — their friends had had the same idea! Nicky, Violet, and Paulina threw on some clothes and hurried to meet the other mouselets. Together they **HEADED** down to the beach.

But when they arrived, the Thea Sisters found a **bitter** surprise waiting for them.

"Moldy Brie on a baguette!" exclaimed Pam, **WIDE-EYED** with shock. "What happened?"

The mouselets couldn't believe the sight

before them. The **beach** was completely covered by debris washed in from the sea!

Craig and Shen *RAN* to meet them.

"Mouselets, I'm so glad you're here," said Craig. "Last night there was an enormouse **sea storm**."

"We did what we could to protect the nest," said Shen, "but as you can see, the beach is in **terrible** condition."

How terrible!

Come on!

"So what do we do?" asked Paulina. She was **discouraged**. Broken logs, heaps of seaweed, branches, and other debris from the sea storm cluttered the **shoreline**. There was no way newborn sea turtles would be able to **CROSS** the beach safely. It was just too big a mess!

"Maybe if we get right to work, we can **clean** it up a bit," Violet suggested.

"I love your spirit, Vi, but we'll never

What can we do?

be able to do it," said Nicky, shaking her snout. "Look at this place! It's a disaster. Even if everyone pitches in, it would take **TOO LONG** . . ."

There was a moment of silence. No one knew what to say.

Finally, Pam squeaked up. "Okay, this is it. We've got to think of something. No idea is too **CRAZY**. After everything we've done to protect these turtles, we can't let them down now!"

There was another moment of silence as all the young rodents tried to think of a way to get the beach clear before nightfall.

We can think of something!

"Maybe . . ." Shen began. Then he shook his snout. "**FORGET IT**. It would never work."

Just then a big smile spread across Colette's snout. "Nicky is right," she said eXCiteDLy. "Alone, we'll never be able to **clean up** the beach in time for the eggs to hatch. But we're not the only ones who care about the turtle nest. Think back for a minute. A few days ago, when we first learned about the seaweed **EMERGENCY**, all we had to do was ask the fishermice. They immediately agreed to help us with the **floating** barrier!"

"That's true," reflected Shen.

"So let's try to get as many rodents **INVOLVED** as we can! We can ask everyone on the island to *help*," Colette replied.

THEA SISTERS CALLING . . .

The Thea Sisters, Craig, and Shen immediately returned to Mouseford, where they told their friends about the **sea storm** and Colette's idea.

"But how can we get out word that we **NEED** everyone to help?" asked Mike.

"Simple," responded Pam. "Let's make flyers!"

"Great idea, Pam," said Paulina. "I'll also post it on the school blog." She opened her laptop and began typing FURIOUSLY.

"And I'll work the phones," said Colette, pulling out her MousePhone. "I'm going to send a group text to the whole school!"

While Paulina and Colette worked the Internet, the rest of the **students** began designing FLYERS. Half an hour later, they'd photocopied a stack of papers that read *Seashell Beach Needs You! Help Us Clean It Up!*

Groups of students *scattered* through town to distribute them.

"Come help us! We'll see you this afternoon at Seashell Beach," EXCLAIMED Violet, pawing a **PURPLE** flyer to a family.

"I don't know if I can help you **clean**," a young mouseling told her seriously. "I promised my grandfather I would go visit him."

"It's okay, you have an important **obligation**," said Violet, smiling. "I'm sure that the **TURTLES** will understand. Unless . . . perhaps your grandfather would like to come help, too?"

"Sure!" the little mouseling replied.

Meanwhile, Mike was filming the Thea Sisters as they distributed the **FLYERS**,

and he realized the importance of their work. If the sea **turtle hatchlings** made it, it would really be thanks to the tenderhearted determination of those fabumouse *five friends*!

WHALE ISLAND RESPONDS

That afternoon, for the second time that day, Seashell Beach held disappointment for the Thea Sisters. When they reached the beach with Mike and their FRIENDS from the academy, the mouselets found the exact opposite of what they'd hoped: the beach was deserted!

"But . . . no one came!" exclaimed Violet. She was totally down in the snout.

"I'm sorry, mouselets," said Colette in a small squeak. "I was so SURE everyone would come help!"

"Now what do we do?" asked Nicky.

"I don't know," Paulina replied. "How can we do this all by ourselves? Maybe we should just GIVE UP." She slumped on a *log* with her snout in her paws.

Her friends looked so **down**, Pam tried to cheer them up. "Come on, mouselings! The Thea Sisters don't give up hope so easily. Remember, we can count on one another. Friends together, mice forever!"

Come on, sisters, don't give up!

Look . . .

"**ACTUALLY**," Mike began, pointing into the **distance**, "I'd say you've got a lot more friends than you realize."

The Thea Sisters **LOOKED** toward

Done!

Bring it over here!

the end of the beach. What they saw took their BREATH away. Everyone was there: their friends from the academy, the **fishermice** from the port, and dozens and dozens of Whale Island residents!

The mouselets ran to meet the crowd.

"Thank you all for coming!" exclaimed Nicky.

Good job, Zoe!

"An emergency is an EMERGENCY," said Tamara, who had closed her store, the Thrifty Rat, for the occasion.

"You didn't really think we would leave you ALONE, did you?" joked Professor Van Kraken.

"Well, actually . . ." said Paulina, "I have to admit that when we saw that there wasn't anyone here, we almost lost hope."

Great work, little one!

Just then the YOUNG mouseling Violet and Mike had seen that morning emerged from the CROWD.

"Did you see, Miss?" he asked sweetly. "I came to clean the

beach for the little turtles . . . and I brought my grandfather!"

"Thank you so much. We can use **everyone's** help!" said Violet. "So come on — shake a tail. Let's get to **WORK**!"

UNITY IS STRENGTH!

Cleaning up Seashell Beach was hard work, but it was work done in a **jolly** atmosphere. It was as if a big family had gathered on the beach for a reunion. Everyone worked together as **cheerfully** as a scurry of chipmunks.

This bag is full!

"Look," said Nicky as she waited for Pam to haul away some old **branches**, "the Ruby Crew is down there!"

Connie, Zoey, and Alicia were mixed in with the crowd, and they were busily clearing the **sand**.

"That's great," said Colette. "The Golden Dragonflies are finally helping **NATURE** for real!"

The **ONLY** one missing was Ruby. After her fight with the **STORM**, she was in bed fighting off a terrible **cold**.

Ugh . . .

The time **flew**, and in the space of a few hours, the beach was **clean** and **clear**.

Only a few branches remained.

"Professor, I'd say we're done," said Nicky, wiping away a **TEAR**.

"I'm **proud** of you," Professor Van Kraken said, smiling at his students. "Now we just have to wait for these **BABIES** to find their way out."

Midge Whale strode onto the **beach**, lugging a basket full of Swiss-cheese

sandwiches. "Great job, everyone! It's time for a **HARD-EARNED** snack," she called.

"Yay! I'm as hungry as a tomcat at feeding time," exclaimed Pam, *scurrying* toward Midge.

In her rush, she tripped over a **LOG** and bumped into Elly, who fell onto Paulina, who smacked into Shen, making him **tumble** and roll all the way down the beach!

"Jumping tuna fish!" muttered Pam with her snout in the sand. "Look at the mess I've made now . . ."

Colette, Nicky, and Violet came to lend their friends a **helping** paw.

"After we're done taking care of the turtles," Colette said, while *giggling*, "it'll be time to take care of our friend Pam's **stomach**!"

Huh...?

"You can say that again, Coco." Nicky laughed, **HUGGING** Pamela. "Are you ready for that sandwich?"

"You bet!" Pam replied happily.

WELCOME, TURTLES!

That night, the Thea Sisters, Professor Van Kraken, James Ratteron, and Mike all stayed on **Seashell Beach** waiting for the first **turtles** to appear. The little group brought blankets, thermoses of hot tea, and more sandwiches. They camped in a spot not far from the nest.

There, in silence, everyone watched the sky, which was speckled with thousands of twinkling **stars**. The young rodents didn't turn on their flashlights because the artificial **LIGHT** might confuse the turtles and make them lose their way.

"Look! The sand is moving!" Paulina suddenly whispered.

Everyone **SLOWLY** and silently moved closer to the nest. At the place where the

eggs were buried, a TINY flipper appeared, and then another, and, finally, the **NOSE** of an itty-bitty turtle came out of the sand.

Very slowly, other turtles emerged. The group of spectators watched them scuttle toward the **SHORE** one after another. They were guided by the powerful instinct that called them to their home: the **SEA**.

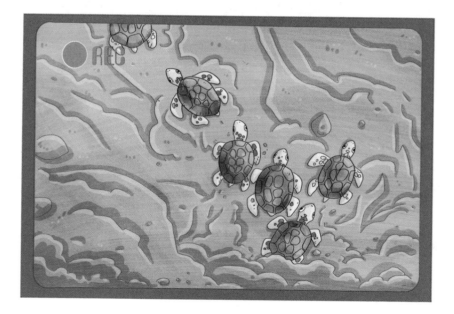

The Thea Sisters and their friends were overcome with awe at the incredible sight before them.

"Welcome, **LITTLE ONES** . . ." whispered Mike as he filmed the brood.

James Ratteron put a paw on his shoulder.

"You're doing a **GREAT** job, Mike. Like these babies, you've found your path!"

Mike **SMILED** from behind his video camera.

"What do you think?" whispered Paulina. "When they grow up, do you think they will remember this place and return?"

"Yes," said Nicky. "And Whale Island will remember them, too!"

Don't miss any of these exciting *Thea Sisters* adventures!

Thea Stilton and the Dragon's Code

Thea Stilton and the Mountain of Fire

Thea Stilton and the Ghost of the Shipwreck

Thea Stilton and the Secret City

Thea Stilton and the Mystery in Paris

Thea Stilton and the Cherry Blossom Adventure

Thea Stilton and the Star Castaways

Thea Stilton: Big Trouble in the Big Apple

Thea Stilton and the Ice Treasure

Thea Stilton and the Secret of the Old Castle

Thea Stilton and the Blue Scarab Hunt

Thea Stilton and the Prince's Emerald

Thea Stilton and the Mystery on the Orient Express

Thea Stilton and the Dancing Shadows

Thea Stilton and the Legend of the Fire Flowers

Thea Stilton and the Spanish Dance Mission

Thea Stilton and the Journey to the Lion's Den

Thea Stilton and the Great Tulip Heist

Thea Stilton and the Chocolate Sabotage

Thea Stilton and the Missing Myth

Thea Stilton and the Lost Letters

Thea Stilton and the Tropical Treasure

Thea Stilton and the Hollywood Hoax

Thea Stilton and the Madagascar Madness

Don't miss any of these Mouseford Academy adventures!

#1 Drama at Mouseford

#2 The Missing Diary

#3 Mouselets in Danger

#4 Dance Challenge

#5 The Secret Invention

#6 A Mouseford Musical

#7 Mice Take the Stage

#8 A Fashionable Mystery

#9 The Mysterious Love Letter

#10 A Dream on Ice

#11 Lights, Camera, Action!

#12 Mice on the Runway

#13 Sea Turtle Rescue

#14 The Secret Notebook

Be sure to read all my fabumouse adventures!

#1 Lost Treasure of the Emerald Eye

#2 The Curse of the Cheese Pyramid

#3 Cat and Mouse in a Haunted House

#4 I'm Too Fond of My Fur!

#5 Four Mice Deep in the Jungle

#6 Paws Off, Cheddarface!

#7 Red Pizzas for a Blue Count

#8 Attack of the Bandit Cats

#9 A Fabumouse Vacation for Geronimo

#10 All Because of a Cup of Coffee

#11 It's Halloween, You 'Fraidy Mouse!

#12 Merry Christmas, Geronimo!

#13 The Phantom of the Subway

#14 The Temple of the Ruby of Fire

#15 The Mona Mousa Code

#16 A Cheese-Colored Camper

#17 Watch Your Whiskers, Stilton!

#18 Shipwreck on the Pirate Islands

#19 My Name Is Stilton, Geronimo Stilton

#20 Surf's Up, Geronimo!

#21 The Wild, Wild West

#22 The Secret of Cacklefur Castle

A Christmas Tale

#23 Valentine's Day Disaster

#24 Field Trip to Niagara Falls

#25 The Search for Sunken Treasure

#26 The Mummy with No Name

#27 The Christmas Toy Factory

#28 Wedding Crasher

#29 Down and Out Down Under

#30 The Mouse Island Marathon

#31 The Mysterious Cheese Thief

Christmas Catastrophe

#32 Valley of the Giant Skeletons

#33 Geronimo and the Gold Medal Mystery

#34 Geronimo Stilton, Secret Agent

#35 A Very Merry Christmas

#36 Geronimo's Valentine

#37 The Race Across America

#38 A Fabumouse School Adventure

#39 Singing Sensation

#40 The Karate Mouse

#41 Mighty Mount Kilimanjaro

#42 The Peculiar Pumpkin Thief

#43 I'm Not a Supermouse!

#44 The Giant Diamond Robbery

#45 Save the White Whale!

#46 The Haunted Castle

Geronimo Stilton

#47 Run for the Hills, Geronimo!

#48 The Mystery in Venice

#49 The Way of the Samurai

#50 This Hotel Is Haunted!

#51 The Enormouse Pearl Heist

#52 Mouse in Space!

#53 Rumble in the Jungle

#54 Get into Gear, Stilton!

#55 The Golden Statue Plot

#56 Flight of the Red Bandit

Special Edition!
The Hunt for the Golden Book

#57 The Stinky Cheese Vacation

#58 The Super Chef Contest

#59 Welcome to Moldy Manor

Special Edition!
The Hunt for the Curious Cheese

#60 The Treasure of Easter Island

#61 Mouse House Hunter

#62 Mouse Overboard!

Special Edition!
The Hunt for the Secret Papyrus

#63 The Cheese Experiment

#64 Magical Mission

#65 Bollywood Burglary

Special Edition!
The Hunt for the Hundredth Key

#66 Operation: Secret Recipe

Be sure to read all of our magical special edition adventures!

THE KINGDOM OF FANTASY

THE QUEST FOR PARADISE:
THE RETURN TO THE KINGDOM OF FANTASY

THE AMAZING VOYAGE:
THE THIRD ADVENTURE IN THE KINGDOM OF FANTASY

THE DRAGON PROPHECY:
THE FOURTH ADVENTURE IN THE KINGDOM OF FANTASY

THE VOLCANO OF FIRE:
THE FIFTH ADVENTURE IN THE KINGDOM OF FANTASY

THE SEARCH FOR TREASURE:
THE SIXTH ADVENTURE IN THE KINGDOM OF FANTASY

THE ENCHANTED CHARMS:
THE SEVENTH ADVENTURE IN THE KINGDOM OF FANTASY

THE PHOENIX OF DESTINY:
AN EPIC KINGDOM OF FANTASY ADVENTURE

THE HOUR OF MAGIC:
THE EIGHTH ADVENTURE IN THE KINGDOM OF FANTASY

THE WIZARD'S WAND:
THE NINTH ADVENTURE IN THE KINGDOM OF FANTASY

THEA STILTON: THE JOURNEY TO ATLANTIS

THEA STILTON: THE SECRET OF THE FAIRIES

THEA STILTON: THE SECRET OF THE SNOW

THEA STILTON: THE CLOUD CASTLE

THEA STILTON: THE TREASURE OF THE SEA

WHALE ISLAND

MAP OF WHALE ISLAND

1. Falcon Peak
2. Observatory
3. Mount Landslide
4. Solar Energy Plant
5. Ram Plain
6. Very Windy Point
7. Turtle Beach
8. Beachy Beach
9. Mouseford Academy
10. Kneecap River
11. Mariner's Inn
12. Port
13. Squid House
14. Town Square
15. Butterfly Bay
16. Mussel Point
17. Lighthouse Cliff
18. Pelican Cliff
19. Nightingale Woods
20. Marine Biology Lab
21. Hawk Woods
22. Windy Grotto
23. Seal Grotto
24. Seagulls Bay
25. Seashell Beach

THANKS FOR READING, AND GOOD-BYE UNTIL OUR NEXT ADVENTURE!

Thea Sisters